Billie B. Brown

www.BillieBBrownBooks.com

Billie B. Brown Books

The Bad Butterfly
The Soccer Star
The Midnight Feast
The Second-best Friend
The Extra-special Helper
The Beautiful Haircut
The Big Sister
The Spotty Vacation
The Birthday Mix-up
The Secret Message
The Little Lie
The Best Project

The Deep End
The Copycat Kid
The Night Fright
The Bully Buster
The Missing Tooth
The Book Buddies
The Grumpy Neighbor
The Honey Bees
The Hat Parade
The Best Day Ever
The Pocket Money Blues
The Cutest Pet Ever

First American Edition 2023
Kane Miller, A Division of EDC Publishing

Text copyright © 2012 Sally Rippin
Illustration copyright © 2012 Aki Fukuoka
Series design copyright © 2023 Hardie Grant Children's Publishing
Original Title: Billie B Brown: *The Pocket Money Blues*
First published in Australia by Hardie Grant Children's Publishing

Library of Congress Control Number: 2022945288
Printed and bound in the United States of America
1 2 3 4 5 6 7 8 9 10

ISBN: 978-1-68464-669-2

Billie B. Brown

The Pocket Money Blues

By Sally Rippin

Illustrated by Aki Fukuoka

Kane Miller

A DIVISION OF EDC PUBLISHING

Chapter One

Billie B. Brown has three long-haired dolls, one big teddy bear and one purple pony. Do you know what the "B" in Billie B. Brown stands for?

Bunny Babies.

Billie B. Brown really, really wants a Bunny Baby toy. Bunny Babies have soft fur and big sparkly eyes. Bunny Babies even have their own TV show.

Every single girl in Billie's class has a Bunny Baby. Except for Billie.

One purple pony

One big teddy bear

Three long-haired dolls

"Please, please, please can I have a Bunny Baby?" Billie asks her mom.

"No, Billie," says her mom. "I've already said that you'll have to wait until Christmas."

"But that's ages away!" Billie says. "I can't wait until then."

"Why don't you try saving up for one yourself?" Billie's dad says. "You already have some money in your piggy bank. Maybe you can do a few jobs to earn some more?"

"OK!" says Billie. "What can I do?"

"Well, you could sort through your toys," Billie's mom says. "You can throw out any that are broken and give away the ones that you are too big for."

Billie frowns. "That's not a job! I mean like sweeping leaves or mowing."

"You're too young to mow the lawn," says Billie's dad.

"But you can sweep the driveway. The brooms are in the back shed."

"Cool!" Billie says. She runs out the back door.

Billie sees someone peeking over the back fence. You know who it is, don't you? That's right. It's Jack! Jack is Billie's best friend. He lives next door.

"Hey, Billie!" calls Jack.

"Do you want to come
over and play cricket?

I've made a bat out of some old wood and I've drawn stumps on the fence with chalk. Come and see!"

Billie giggles. "Not now, Jack," she says. "I have to sweep the driveway."

"Can I help?" says Jack.

"Sure," says Billie. "Thanks!"

Billie and Jack work hard sweeping the leaves off the driveway. Jack holds open the garbage bag and Billie scoops the leaves in.

When they have finished,
Billie's dad comes outside
to admire their work.

"Hey, that looks great!"
Billie's dad says. He gives
her some coins.

"Thanks, Dad!" says Billie.

She and Jack have
done a good day's work.
Jack goes home.

Billie runs up to her
bedroom to put the
money in her piggy bank.
Billie is very **excited**.
Soon she will have
enough money for her
very own Bunny Baby!

Chapter Two

The next day after school, Billie asks her dad if he has another job for her.

Billie's mom calls out from the kitchen.

"How about sorting
through your toys?"

"Mo-om!" says Billie.

"The car needs washing,"
Billie's dad says.
"It's a big job, though.
Do you think you
can do it?"

"Of course!" says Billie.
She runs outside.

Billie gets
one bucket
of soapy water
and one
bucket of
clean water.

Jack is sitting on his
front step. "Hey, Billie,"
he calls. "Do you want to
play cricket now?"

"I can't," says Billie. "I have to wash the car."

"Can I help?" says Jack.

"Sure," says Billie. "Thanks!"

Billie washes the car with a big sponge. Jack rinses off the soap. It is hard work, but Billie and Jack have fun.

As the car gets cleaner,
Billie and Jack get dirtier.
Soon the car is sparkling.
Billie and Jack are very
tired and very grubby.
Time for a bath, don't
you think?

"Good job!" says Billie's dad. He gives Billie some more coins.

After her bath, Billie flops down on her bed to count her money. She has earned lots today, but she still needs more to buy her Bunny Baby. Doing jobs is very tiring! Billie needs another plan.

Just then Billie's mom knocks on her door. "How about a glass of lemonade, honey?" she says. "You've worked hard today."

This gives Billie an idea. A super-duper idea! Can you guess what she is thinking?

"Thanks!" Billie says to her mom. She gulps down the lemonade. "Now I have to go see Jack!"

Billie runs outside and squeezes through the hole in the fence into Jack's backyard.

Jack is sitting at the
kitchen table with
his mom.

"Hey, Jack!" Billie says.
"I've got a plan that will
earn us *heaps* of money."

Billie looks at Jack's mom.
"We'll need lemons,"
she says. "Lots of them!
Can we please pick some
from your lemon tree?"

"Sure," says Jack's mom.
"Let me guess. You
want to make lemonade,
right?"

"Right!" says Billie.

"A lemonade stand!" Jack laughs. "That's a great idea. Let's make some posters."

Billie grins. "Good idea." She feels very **happy**. She will have enough money to buy her Bunny Baby soon.

Chapter Three

The next day is Saturday.

Billie gets up early.

She and Jack pick all the

ripe lemons off the tree

in his backyard. Jack's

mom helps them mix the

lemon juice with water and sugar. Soon they have three big pitchers of delicious lemonade.

Billie and Jack set up a small table on the sidewalk outside their houses. Jack's mom weeds the front yard. Billie and Jack sell cups of lemonade to people walking past.

Mrs. Wattle from across
the street buys four cups.
She must be very thirsty!
She even lets Billie and
Jack keep the change.

By lunchtime all the lemonade is gone. Billie and Jack run upstairs to Billie's room. They add the money from the lemonade stand to the money from Billie's piggy bank.

"I need one more job," says Billie. "Then I'll have enough money to buy a Bunny Baby. Oh, I can't wait!"

"What?" says Jack. "I don't want a Bunny Baby.
I don't even *like* Bunny Babies. They're silly."

"They are not!" says Billie. "I've been working hard all week to buy one."

"I've been working hard, too!" says Jack. "So half that money should be mine.

And I don't want to buy
a Bunny Baby. I want to
buy something that we
both want."

Billie frowns. Jack doesn't
understand. She *has* to
have a Bunny Baby.

All the girls have a
Bunny Baby except her.
Bunny Babies are the best!

"Well, I didn't
ask you to
help me!" Billie
says gruffly. "Did I?"

Jack gasps. "You're *mean*,
Billie!" he says. "And I'm
never helping you do
anything ever again."

He storms out of
her room.

Billie looks down at
her piggy bank. There is
a little part of her that
feels mean. That part wants
to say sorry. But then she'd
have to share the money
with Jack. And then she
wouldn't have enough
to buy her Bunny Baby.

Billie doesn't know what
to do.

Just then Billie's mom
pokes her head through
the doorway.

She is carrying baby
Noah on her hip.
"How are you doing
with your savings?"

"Nearly there," says
Billie quietly. "I think I
just need one more job."

"You could sort through
your toys?" Billie's mom
grins. Then she walks off
to change Noah's diaper.

Billie sighs. She pulls out her toy basket from the cupboard. She sorts the broken toys into one pile. She puts the baby ones in another pile. It seems to take forever. Billie wishes Jack was here to help her. He makes everything fun.

Chapter
Four

That night Billie's mom
tucks her into bed. "Thanks
for sorting through your
toys, Billie," she says.
"How about we go get
your new toy tomorrow?"

"Thanks, Mom," Billie says. But somehow she doesn't feel as **happy** as she thought she would.

The next morning Billie and her mom drive to Westland Shopping Center.

Mom puts Noah into the stroller and they walk through the busy mall.

"Have you got your money, Billie?" her mom asks.

Billie nods. They walk into an enormous toy store as big as a supermarket. When Billie sees all the toys she begins to feel **excited** again.

Billie and her mom walk up and down the aisles until they find the Bunny Babies. There is a spotted one, and a soft pink one. There are ones with sparkly eyes. There is even one dressed up like a princess.

They are all so beautiful. Billie can't decide which one to buy.

"Come on, Billie,"

Billie's mom says.

"Noah is getting restless.

Have you chosen one?"

But the more Billie looks at the Bunny Babies, the harder it is to decide.

She can't help thinking about Jack. She remembers how hard he worked to help her. And suddenly Billie decides she doesn't want a Bunny Baby anymore. Not if Jack doesn't want one.

Then Billie has an idea.

A super-duper idea.

Billie knows
exactly what

she wants to

spend her

pocket money on.

Do you know what she

is thinking?

Billie turns to her mom.

"Um, I think I'll buy something else instead," she says.

"Really?" says Billie's mom, surprised. "What about your Bunny Baby? I thought you really, really wanted one."

"Nah." Billie shrugs. "I can wait until Christmas."

Billie finds what she wants and pays for it. She keeps the box on her lap all the way home.

She can't wait to see Jack's face when she shows him their new cricket set!

Collect them all!

The Bad Butterfly
By Sally Rippin

The Soccer Star
By Sally Rippin

The Midnight Feast
By Sally Rippin

The Second-best Friend
By Sally Rippin

The Extra-special Helper
By Sally Rippin

The Beautiful Haircut
By Sally Rippin

The Big Sister
By Sally Rippin

The Spotty Vacation
By Sally Rippin

The Birthday Mix-up
By Sally Rippin

The Secret Message
By Sally Rippin

The Little Lie
By Sally Rippin

The Best Project
By Sally Rippin

The Deep End
By Sally Rippin

The Copycat Kid
By Sally Rippin

The Night Fright
By Sally Rippin

The Missing Tooth
By Sally Rippin

The Bully Buster
By Sally Rippin

The Grumpy Neighbor
By Sally Rippin

The Hat Parade
By Sally Rippin

The Honey Bees
By Sally Rippin

The Best Day Ever
By Sally Rippin

The Pocket Money Blues
By Sally Rippin

The Cutest Pet Ever
By Sally Rippin

Don't forget the book starring both Jack AND Billie!